THE
Littlest Pumpkin

For my littlest pumpkin, Gabriel
—R.A.H.

For Paris
—B.O.

Text copyright © 2001 by R.A. Herman.
Illustrations copyright © 2001 by Betina Ogden.
All rights reserved. Published by Scholastic Inc.
SCHOLASTIC, CARTWHEEL BOOKS, and associated logos are trademarks and/or registered trademarks of Scholastic Inc.

Library of Congress Cataloging-in-Publication Data

Herman, R.A. (Ronnie Ann)
   The Littlest Pumpkin / by R.A. Herman ; illustrated by Betina Ogden.
      p. cm.
   Summary: One by one, all the other pumpkins are chosen to become jack-o'-lanterns, but even though no one buys the Littlest Pumpkin, her Halloween dreams come true.
   ISBN-13: 978-0-439-29544-4 (pb)   ISBN-10: 0-439-29544-0 (pb)

   [1. Jack-o'-lanterns--Fiction. 2. Halloween--Fiction. 3. Mice--Fiction.] I. Ogden, Betina,
PZ7.H43155 Li 2001
   [E]--dc21   00-054161

30 29 28 27 26 25 24 23   9 10 11 12/0

Printed in the U.S.A.
First printing, September 2001

THE
Littlest Pumpkin

by R.A. Herman • Illustrated by Betina Ogden

SCHOLASTIC INC. Cartwheel ·B·O·O·K·S·®

New York   Toronto   London   Auckland   Sydney
Mexico City   New Delhi   Hong Kong

It was Halloween, and there were 18 pumpkins left at Bartlett's Farm Stand.

The pumpkins looked their very best, because they all
wanted to be taken home and made into jolly jack-o'-lanterns.

The Littlest Pumpkin had the biggest dreams of all. She saw
herself shining in the dark, with ghosts, monsters, witches, and
fairies gathered around her singing a Halloween song. And today
was the day when all her dreams were going to come true.

Maggie dropped by the stand on her way to school, just as it was opening. "I want the biggest pumpkin you have for my class party," she said, looking at the pumpkins on display.

She didn't even glance at the Littlest Pumpkin.

The pumpkin Maggie chose was so big, Mr. Bartlett had to help her put it in her mother's car.

Then the twins arrived.

Jess wanted the roundest, fattest pumpkin.

Jen wanted the tallest, skinniest pumpkin. They both knew exactly what they wanted their jack-o'-lanterns to look like.

Later that morning, Mrs. Garland's class came to the farm stand to buy apples and pumpkins for their Halloween party. The Littlest Pumpkin was very excited when she saw all the children.

"Now, certainly, I will be chosen by someone and made into a jack-o'-lantern," she thought.

But no one chose
the Littlest Pumpkin.

All day long, people came to the farm stand to buy pumpkins.
Mr. Potter ran in to choose a pumpkin for his daughter, Kate.
Poor Kate was home with the flu, but she had drawn pictures for
her dad so he could see exactly what kind of pumpkin she wanted.

Mr. Potter looked at every single pumpkin until he found the
right one.

The sun began to set, and only four pumpkins were left at the farm stand.

One pumpkin had a bruise on its back.

One pumpkin was lumpy and bumpy.

One pumpkin didn't have a stem.

And the last pumpkin was the Littlest Pumpkin.

The Littlest Pumpkin still had big dreams. She would be a beautiful jack-o'-lantern at a Halloween party. She would shine in the dark, with ghosts, monsters, witches, and fairies gathered around her singing a Halloween song.

But while the Littlest Pumpkin was dreaming, Gabe and Mona arrived. They ran up to the four remaining pumpkins. Gabe grabbed the stemless one.

"Perfect," he said. "My jack-o'-lantern is going to wear this hat."

Mona picked up the Littlest Pumpkin. "Oh, how cute!" she said. The Littlest Pumpkin was so happy! All her dreams were going to come true!

"But . . . it's too small for me to carve into a jack-o'-lantern," said Mona, putting it down. Then she picked up the lumpy bumpy one instead. "Now, *this* one is perfect!"

Soon it was dark, and the stars began to sparkle in the sky. Mr. Bartlett was cleaning up. "Oh, please don't close yet," thought the Littlest Pumpkin. "I *must* be a jack-o'-lantern for Halloween."

Suddenly, Mr. Bartlett heard someone calling his name. "Mr. Bartlett! Mr. Bartlett!" It was Sam!

"Please wait," said Sam. "I need a pumpkin for my party tonight."

Mr. Bartlett picked up the bruised pumpkin and told Sam that if he turned it around, it would make a very nice jack-o'-lantern.

Sam agreed, and with that, Mr. Bartlett closed the farm stand.

So there, in the dark on Halloween night, sat the Littlest Pumpkin. She was all alone.

Or so she thought....

For just when the Littlest Pumpkin was sure she was going to be spending Halloween night all alone in the empty farm stand, mice started scurrying around her. They were decorating everything, wearing tiny costumes, and carrying all sorts of Halloween goodies.

And before the Littlest Pumpkin knew what was happening...

...she found herself in the middle of a Halloween party. Mice dressed in costumes were bobbing for cranberries, playing pin-the-tail-on-the-squirrel, and eating cheese and crumbs.

Then, the best thing of all happened....

The Littlest Pumpkin was turned into a
jack-o'-lantern. She was shining in the dark,
with ghosts, monsters, witches, and fairies
gathered around her singing a Halloween song.

All her big dreams had come true on Halloween night.